BIG A

little   a

What begins with A?

Aunt Annie's alligator . . .

. . . . . A . . a . . A

BIG B

little   b

What begins with B?

Barber
baby
bubbles
and a
bumblebee.

9

BIG C

little   c

What begins with C?

Camel on the ceiling
C . . . . c C

BIG D

little   d

David Donald Doo
dreamed
a dozen doughnuts
and
a duck-dog, too.

ABCDE..e..e

ear

egg

elephant

e

e

E

15

BIG F

little   f

F..f.. F

Four fluffy feathers
on a
Fiffer-feffer-feff.

ABCD
EFG

Goat
girl
googoo goggles
G . . . g . . . G

BIG H

little   h

Hungry horse.
Hay.

Hen in a hat.
Hooray !
Hooray !

BIG I

little   i

i.... i.... i

Icabod
is
itchy.

So am I.

BIG J

little   j

What begins with j?

Jerry Jordan's
jelly jar
and jam
begin that way.

BIG K

little　　　k

Kitten. Kangaroo.

26

Kick a kettle.
Kite
and a
king's kerchoo.

BIG L

little   l

Little Lola Lopp.
Left leg.
Lazy lion
licks a lollipop.

BIG M

little   m

Many mumbling mice
are making
midnight music
in the moonlight . . .

mighty nice

31

BIG N

little n

What begins with those?

Nine new neckties
and a nightshirt
and a nose.

O is very useful.
    You use it when you say:
"Oscar's only ostrich
    oiled
    an orange owl today."

ABCD EFG HIJK LMNO...

...P

Painting pink pyjamas.
Policeman in a pail.

Peter Pepper's puppy.
And now
Papa's in the pail.

BIG Q
little q

What begins with Q ?

The quick
Queen of Quincy
and her
quacking quacker-oo.

QUACK
QUACK

41

BIG R
little r

Rosy Robin Ross.

Rosy's going riding
on her
red rhinoceros.

BIG S

little   s

Silly Sammy Slick
sipped six sodas
and got
sick sick sick.

45

T . . . . . T

t . . . . t

What begins with T ?

Ten tired turtles
on a tuttle-tuttle tree.

47

BIG U

little   u

What begins with U?

Uncle Ubb's umbrella
and his
underwear, too.

49

BIG V

little   v

Vera Violet Vinn
 is
very
very
very awful
on her violin.

W . . w . . W

Willy Waterloo
washes Warren Wiggins
who is
washing Waldo Woo.

X is very useful
if your name is
Nixie Knox.
It also
comes in handy
spelling axe
and extra fox.

NIXIE KNOX

BIG Y

little y

A yawning yellow yak.
Young Yolanda Yorgenson
is yelling on his back.

QRS TUV...

W..X Y.. and ....

BIG Z

little z

What begins with Z?

I do.

I am a
Zizzer-Zazzer-Zuzz
as you can
plainly see.

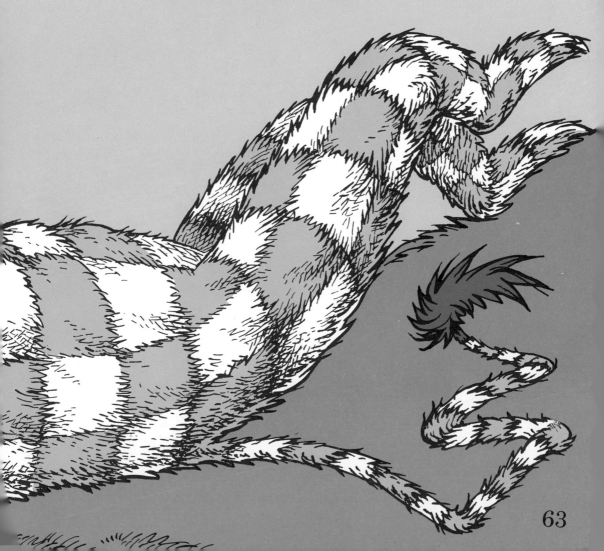

Dr. Seuss™

The more that you **read**,
the more things **you** will know.
The more that you **learn**,
the **more** places you'll go!

– I Can Read With My Eyes Shut!

With over **35 paperbacks to collect** there's a book for all ages and reading abilities, and now there's never been a better time to have **fun** with **Dr.Seuss!** Simply collect 5 tokens from the back of each Dr.Seuss book and send in for your

FREE Dr.Seuss poster

(rrp £3.99)

Send your 5 tokens and a completed voucher to:
Dr. Seuss poster offer, PO Box 142, Horsham, UK, RH13 5FJ (UK residents only)

VOUCHER

Title: Mr ☐   Mrs ☐   Miss ☐   Ms ☐

First Name:_____ Surname: _____

Address:_____

Post Code:_____ E-Mail Address: _____

Date of Birth:_____ Signature of parent/guardian:_____

TICK HERE IF YOU DO NOT WISH TO RECEIVE FURTHER INFORMATION ABOUT CHILDREN'S BOOKS ☐

TERMS AND CONDITIONS: Proof of sending cannot be considered proof of receipt. Not redeemable for cash. Please allow 28 days for delivery. Photocopied tokens not accepted. Offer open to UK only.

Read them **together**, read them **alone**, read them **aloud** and make **reading fun!**
With over **30 wacky stories** to choose from, now it's **easier** than **ever** to find the
right **Dr. Seuss** books for your child – just let the **back cover colour** guide you!

Blue back books
for sharing with your child

Dr. Seuss' ABC
The Foot Book
Hop on Pop
Mr. Brown Can Moo! Can You?
One Fish, Two Fish, Red Fish, Blue Fish
There's a Wocket in my Pocket!

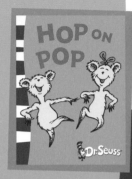

Green back books
for children just beginning to read on their own

And to Think That I Saw It on Mulberry Street
The Cat in the Hat
The Cat in the Hat Comes Back
Fox in Socks
Green Eggs and Ham
I Can Read With My Eyes Shut!
I Wish That I Had Duck Feet
Marvin K. Mooney Will You Please Go Now!
Oh, Say Can You Say?
Oh, the Thinks You Can Think!
Ten Apples Up on Top
Wacky Wednesday
Hunches in Bunches
Happy Birthday to YOU

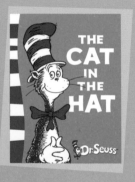

Yellow back books
for fluent readers to enjoy

Daisy-Head Mayzie
Did I Ever Tell You How Lucky You Are?
Dr. Seuss' Sleep Book
Horton Hatches the Egg
Horton Hears a Who!
How the Grinch Stole Christmas!
If I Ran the Circus
If I Ran the Zoo
I Had Trouble in Getting to Solla Sollew
The Lorax
Oh, the Places You'll Go!
On Beyond Zebra
Scrambled Eggs Super!
The Sneetches and other stories
Thidwick the Big-Hearted Moose
Yertle the Turtle and other stories

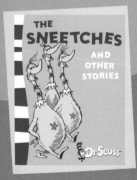